Run, Run!

Written by Alex Lane
Illustrated by Paula Metcalf

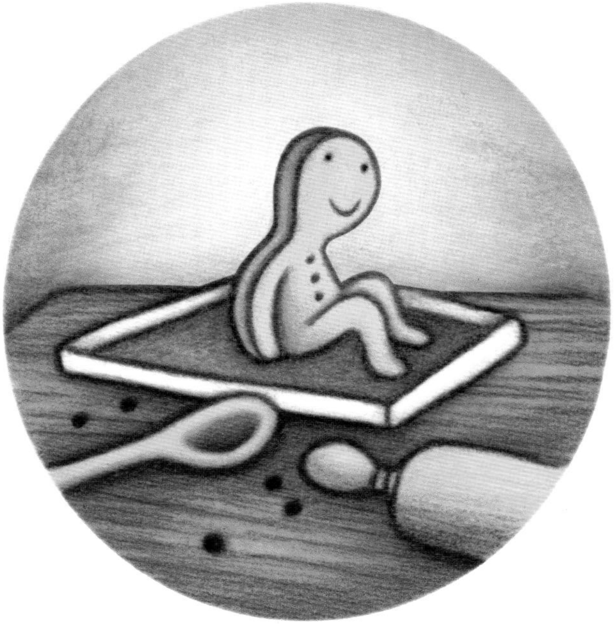

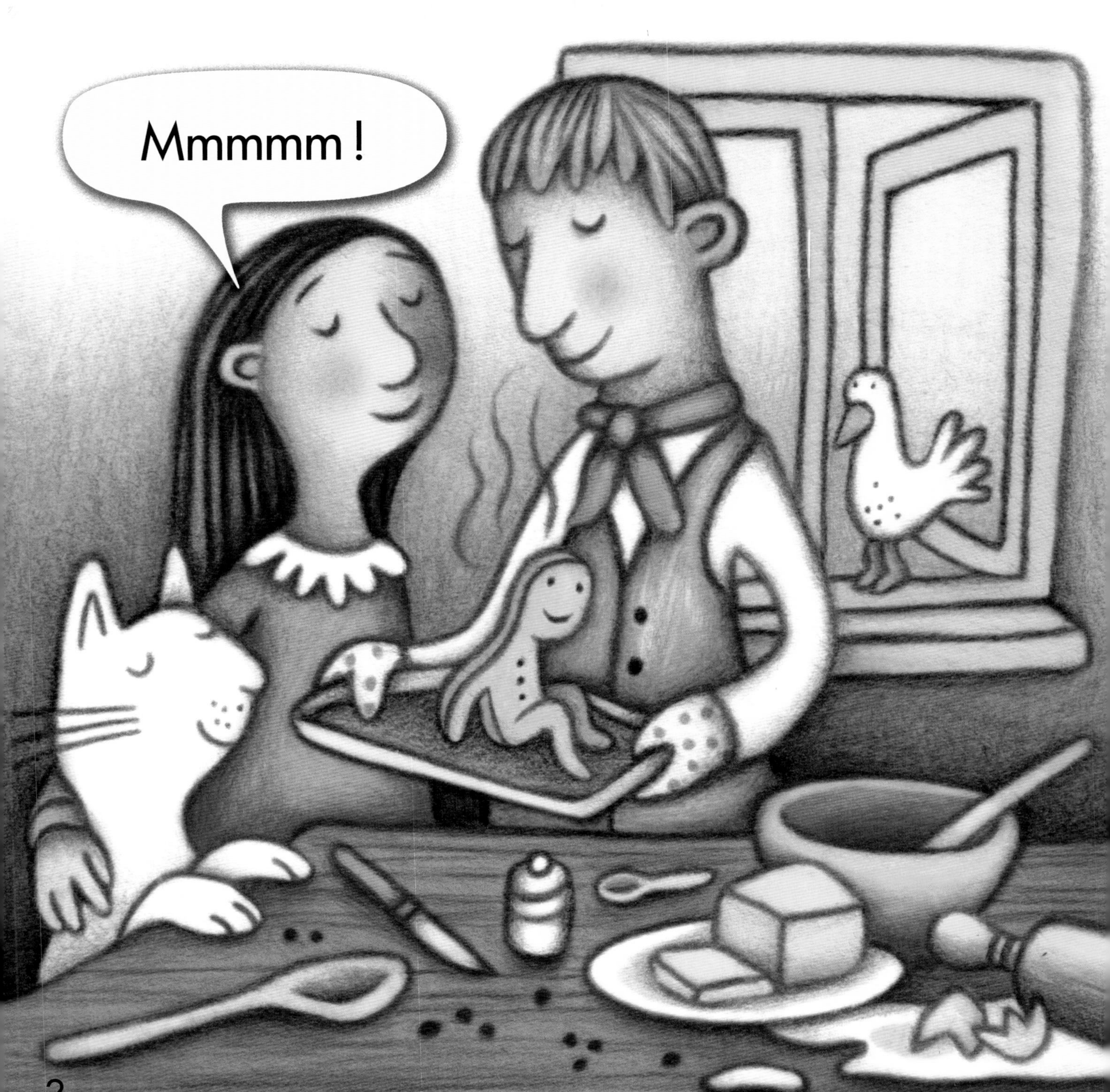
Mmmmm!

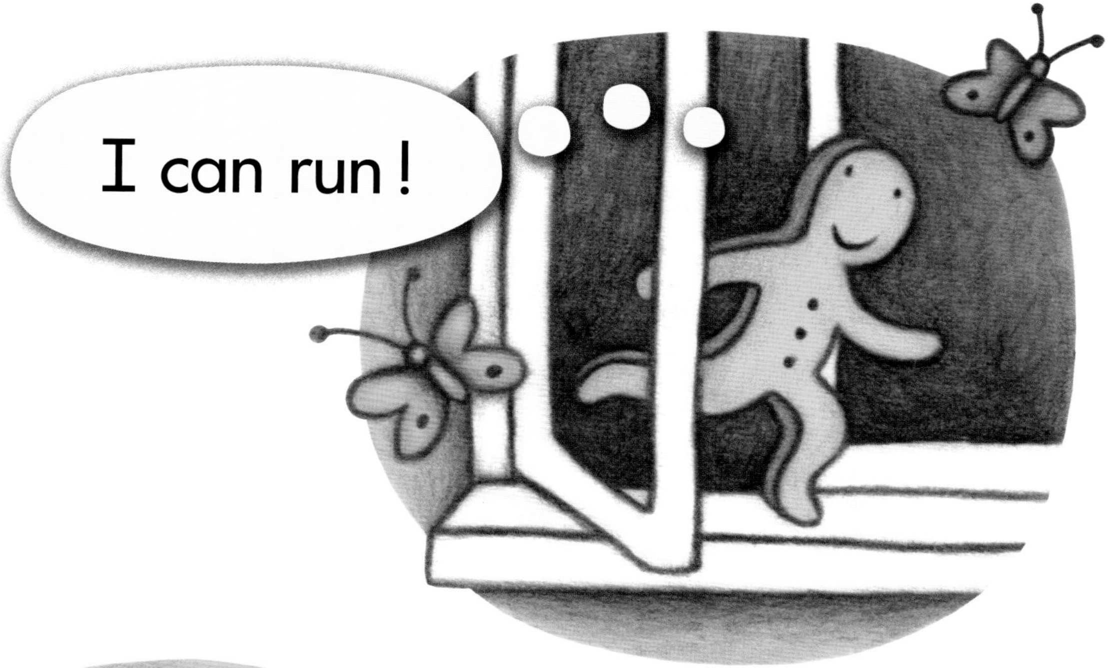
I can run!

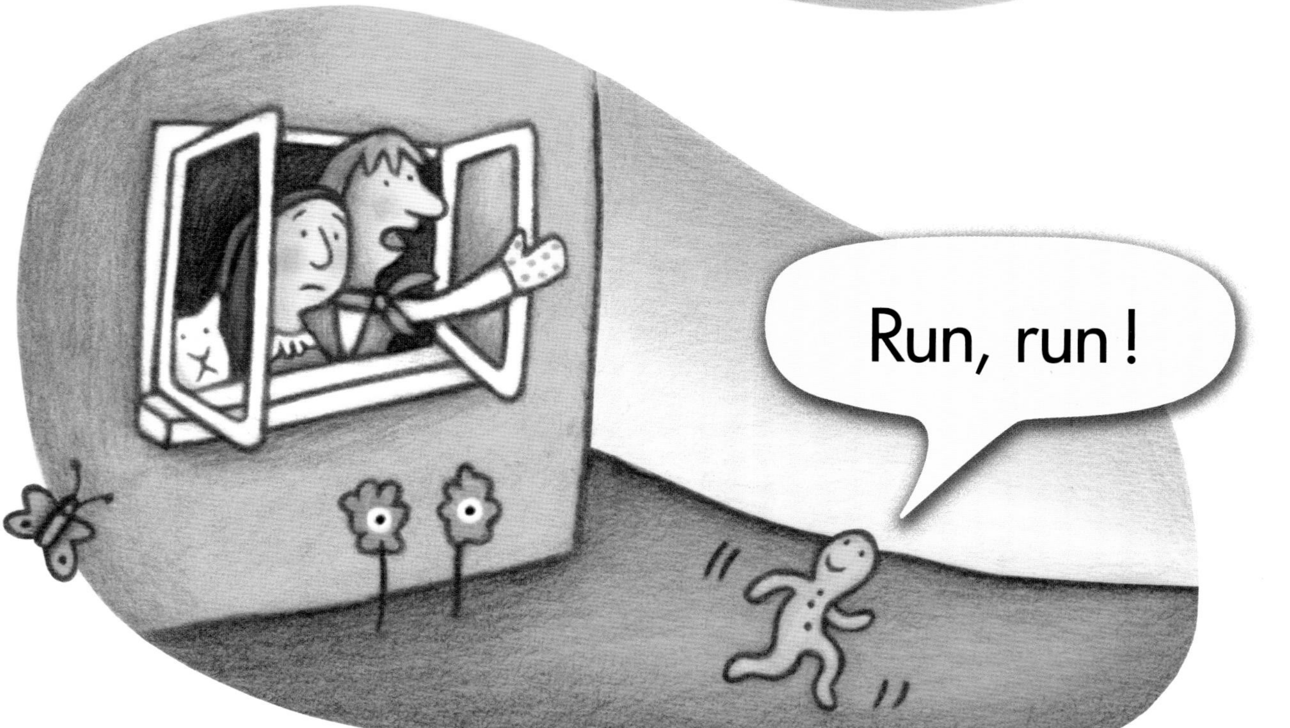
Run, run!

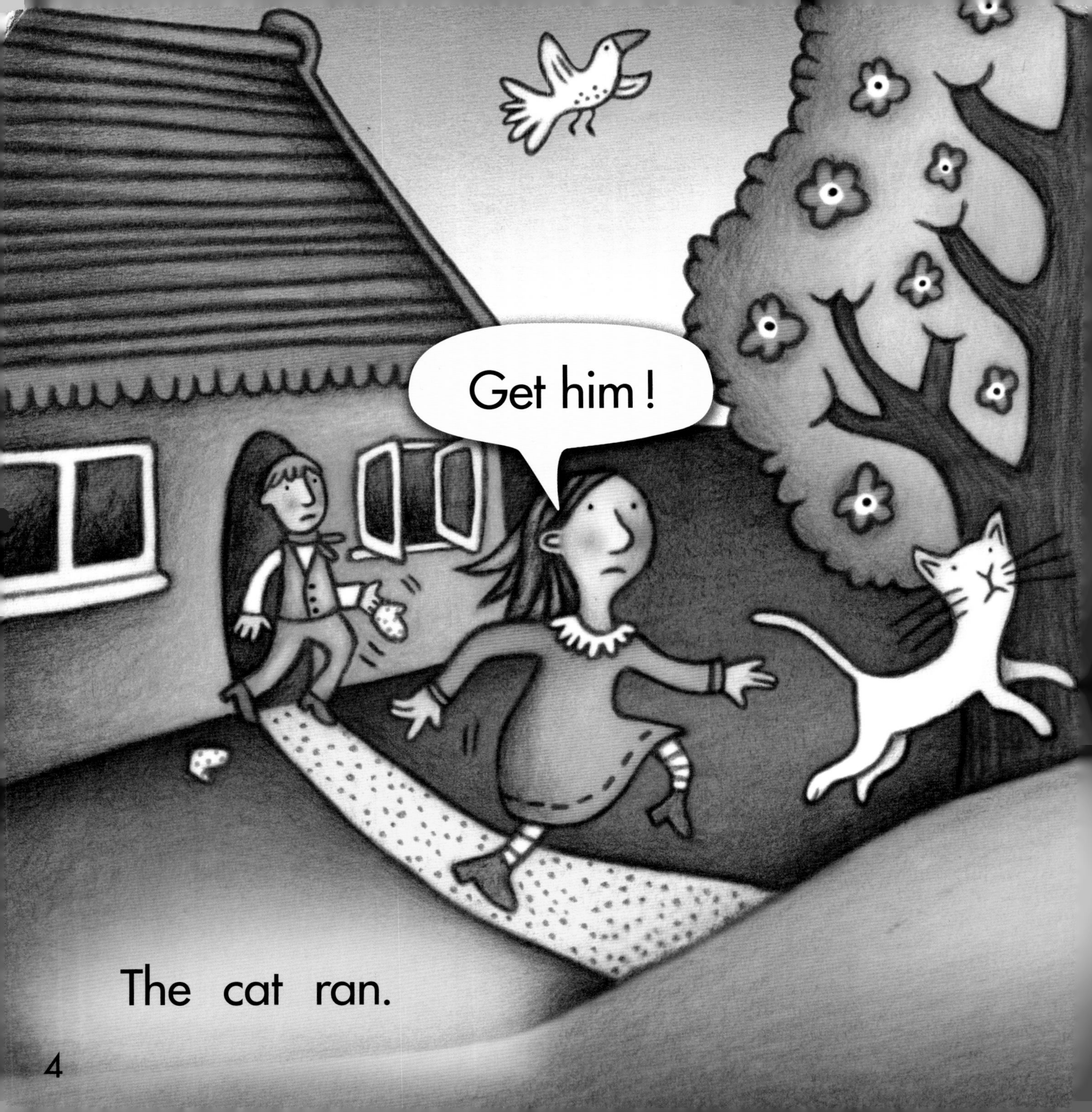

The cat ran.

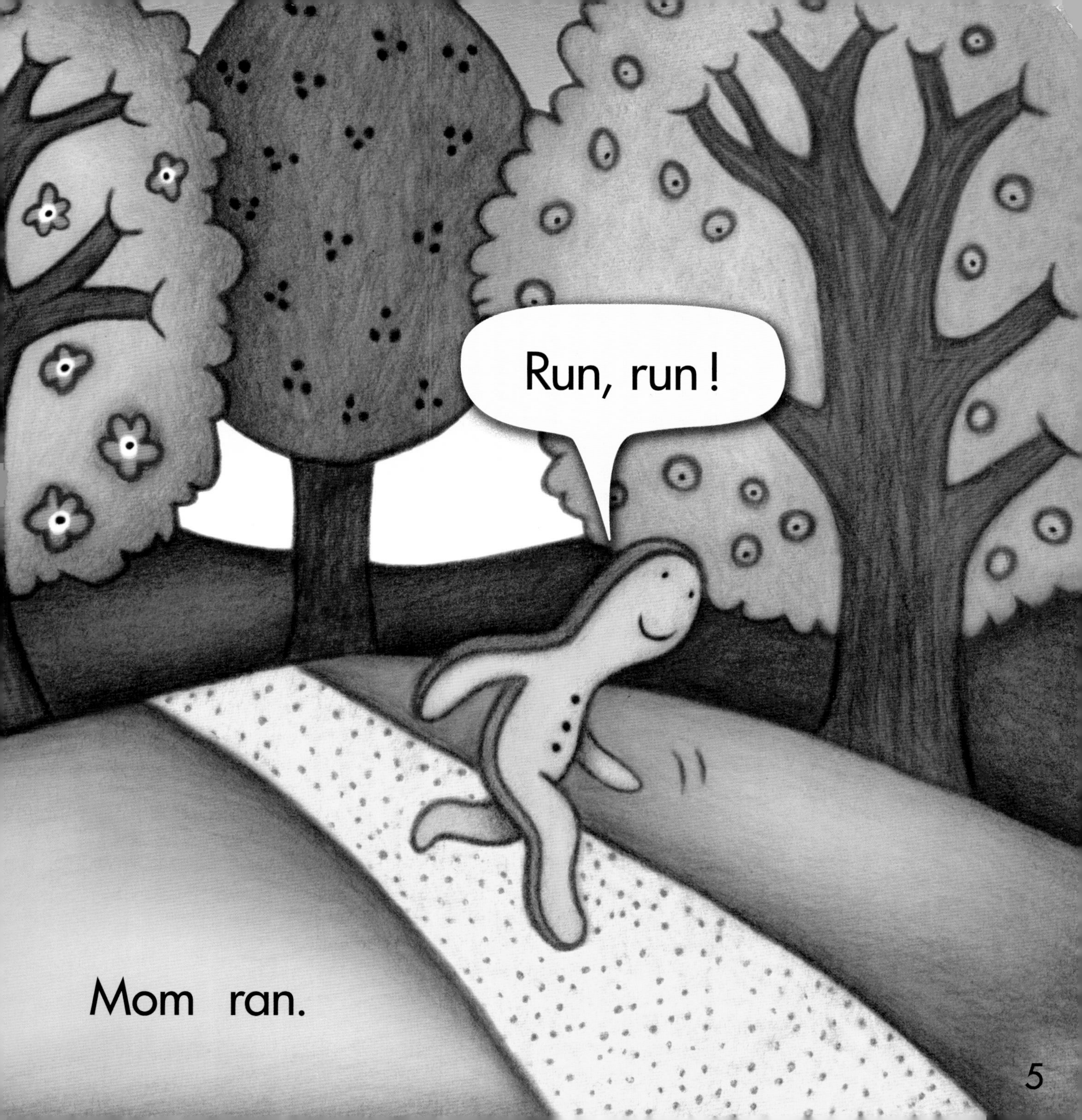

Mom ran.

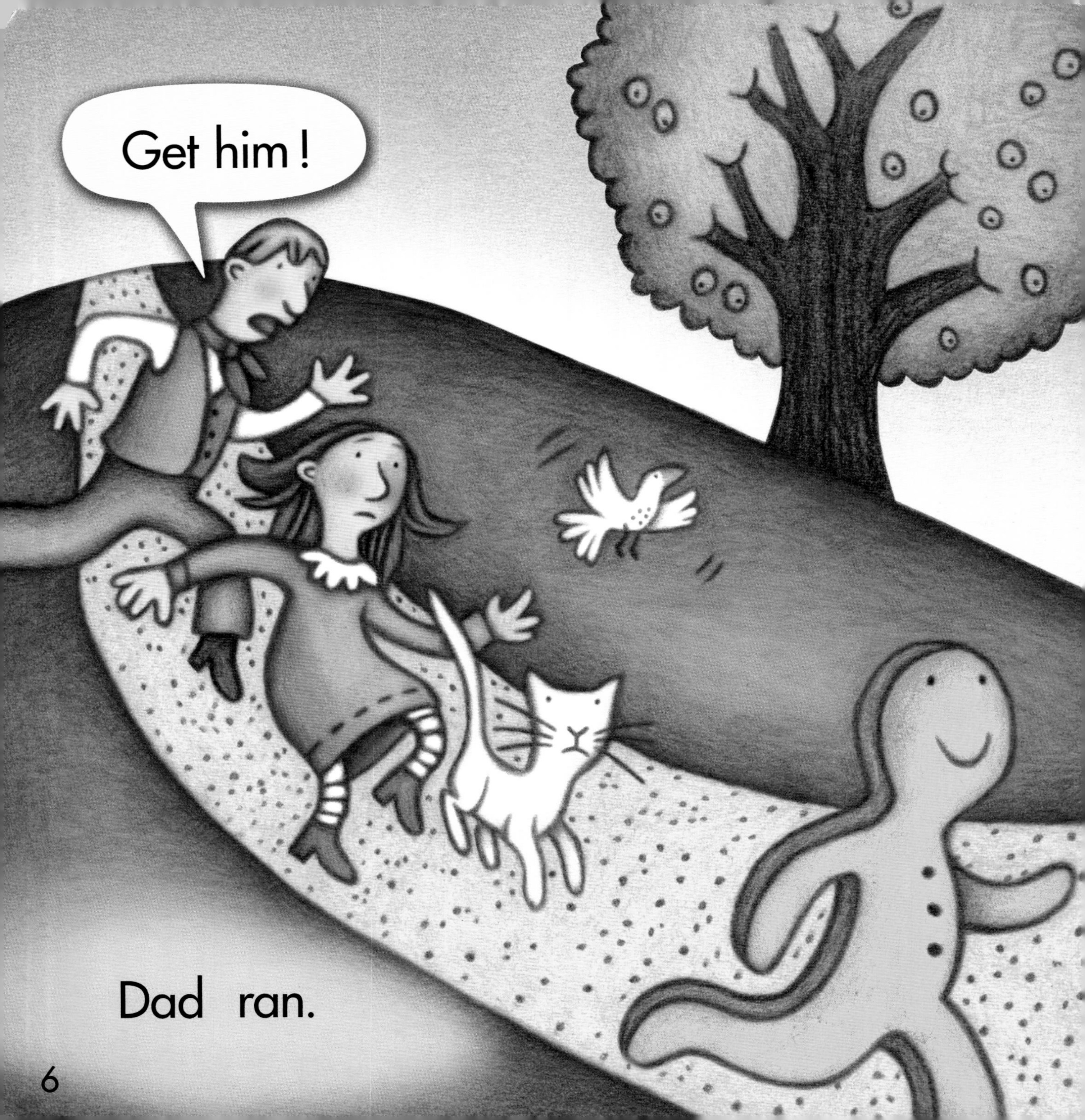

Dad ran.

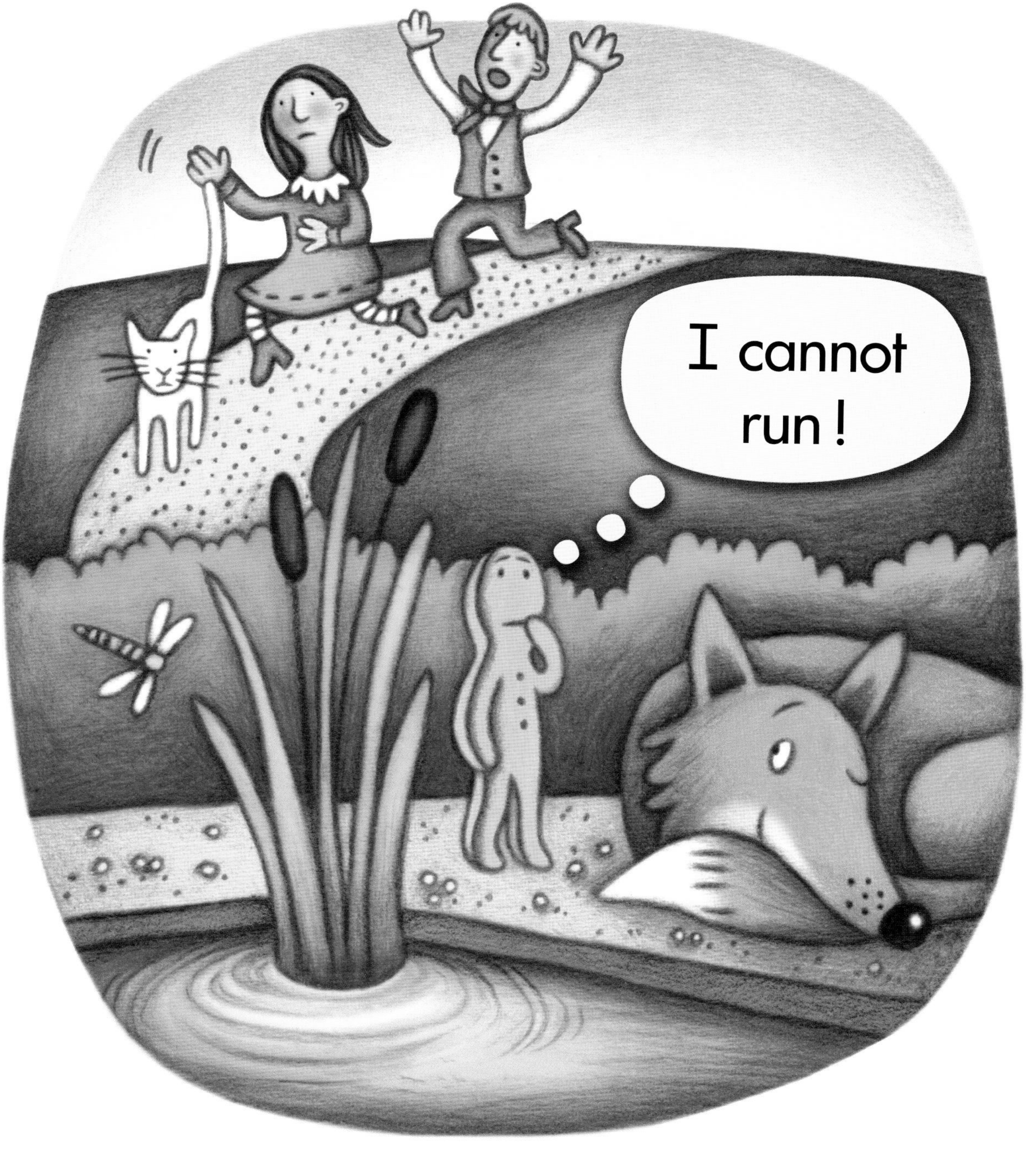
I cannot run !

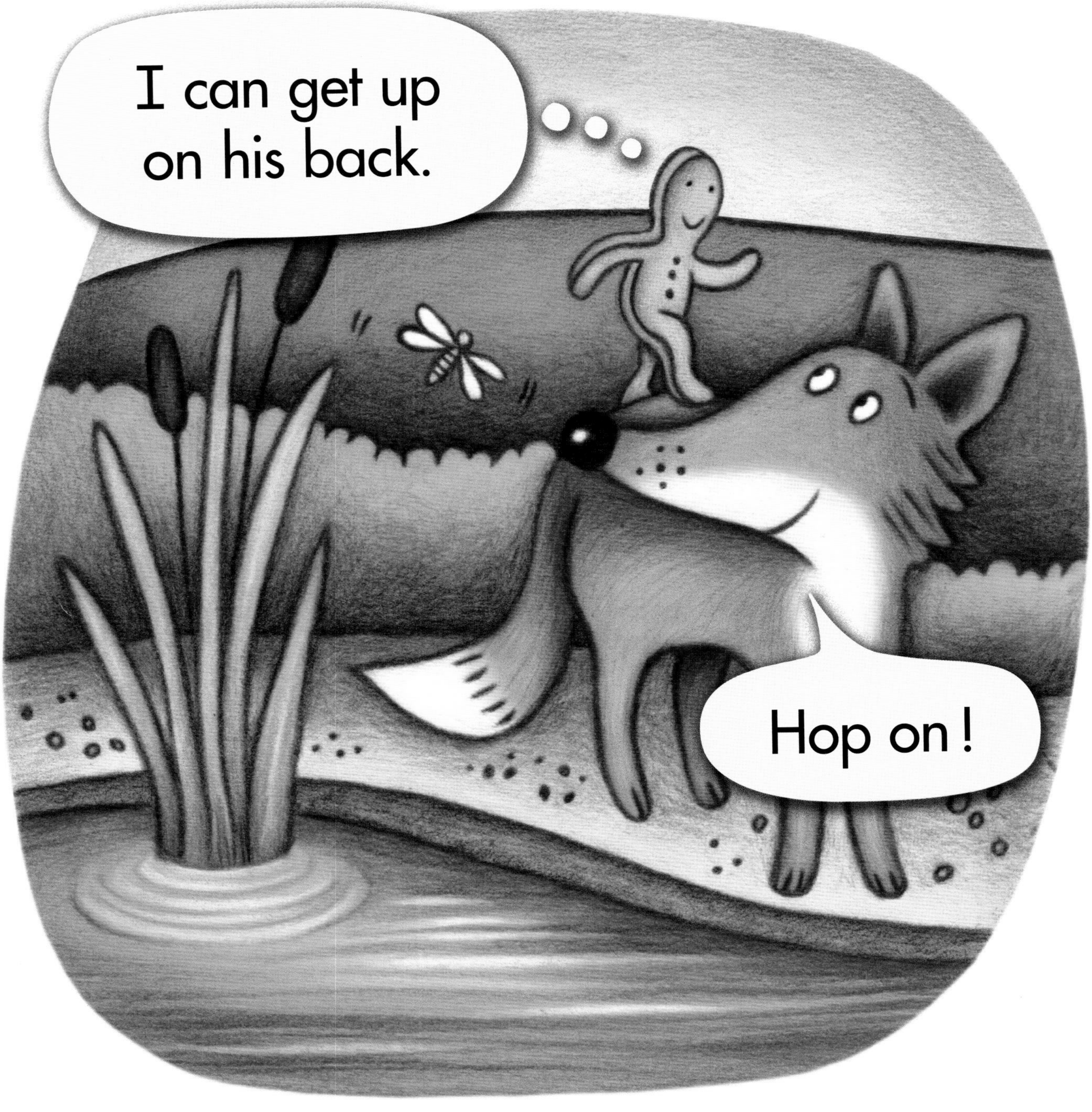
I can get up on his back.
Hop on!

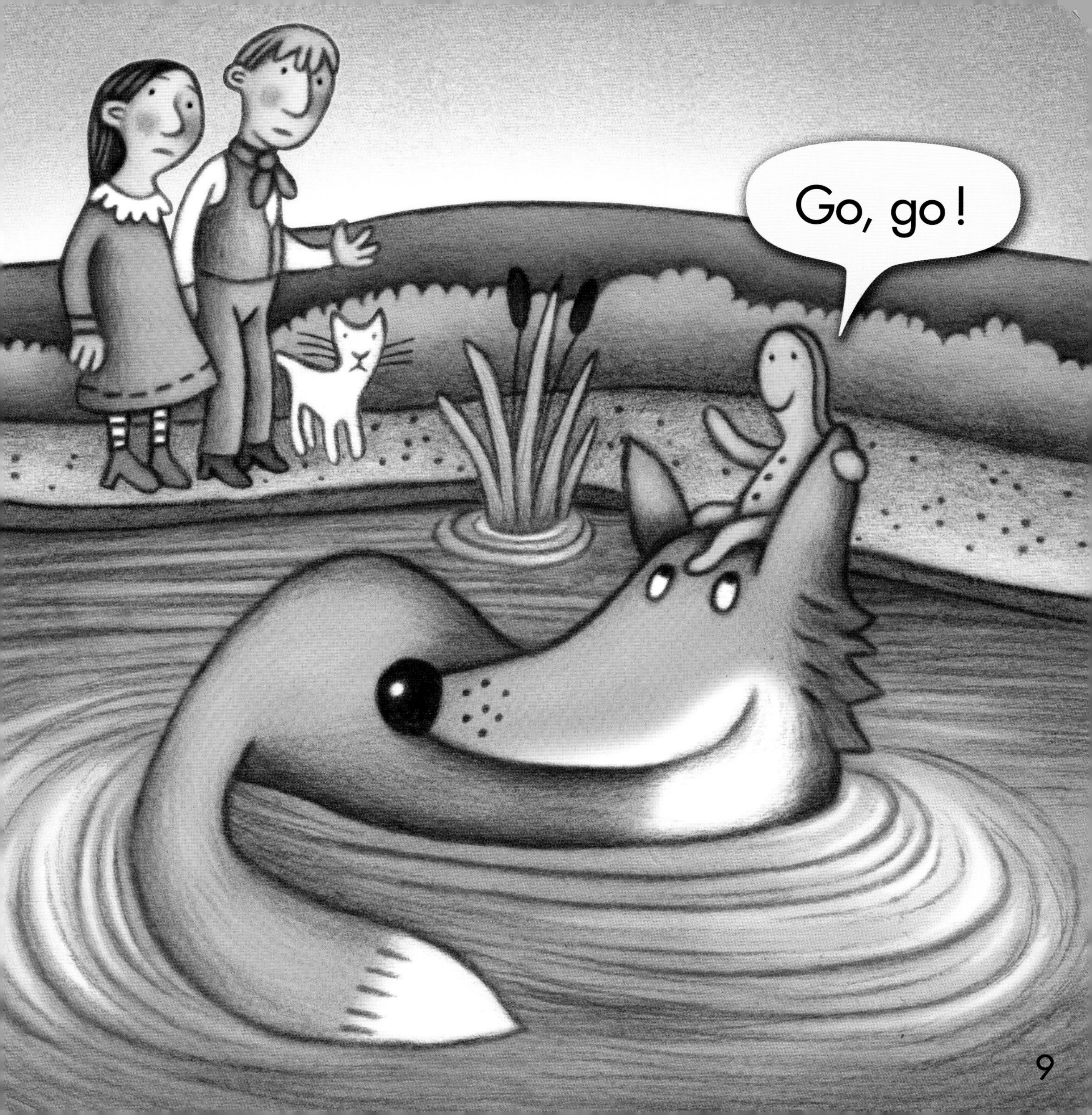
Go, go!

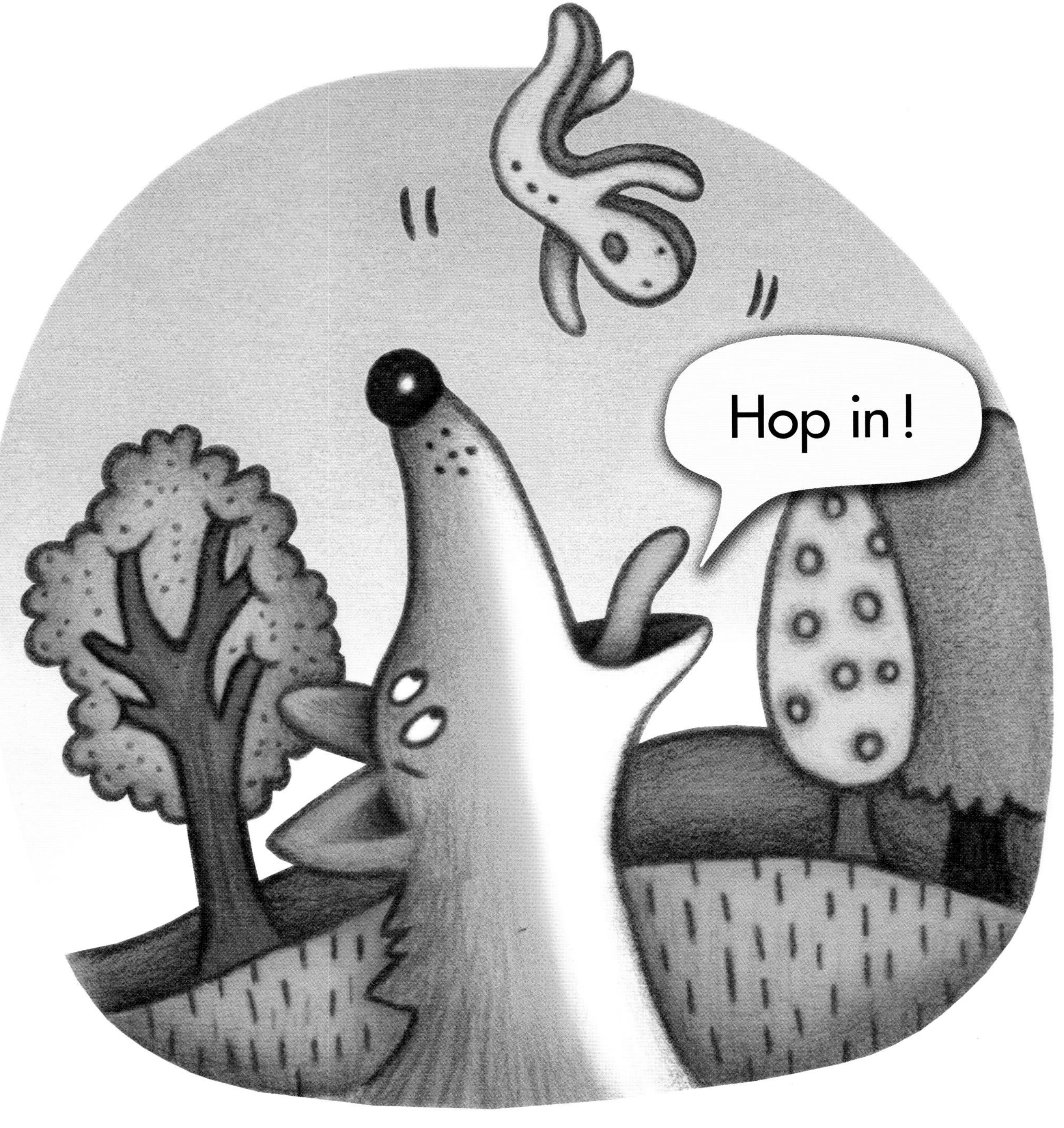
Hop in!

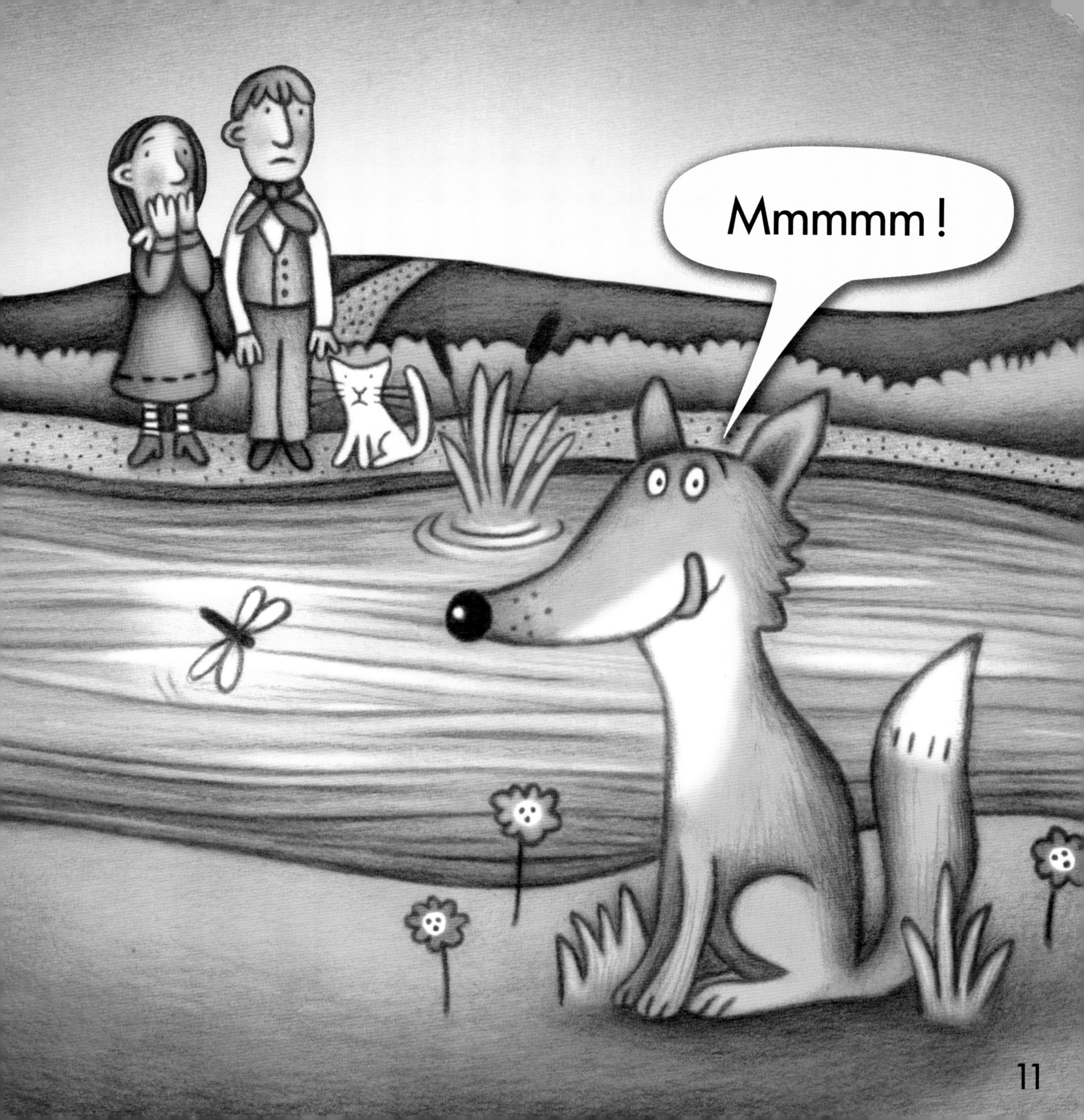
Mmmmm !

Retell the story

Once upon a time ...

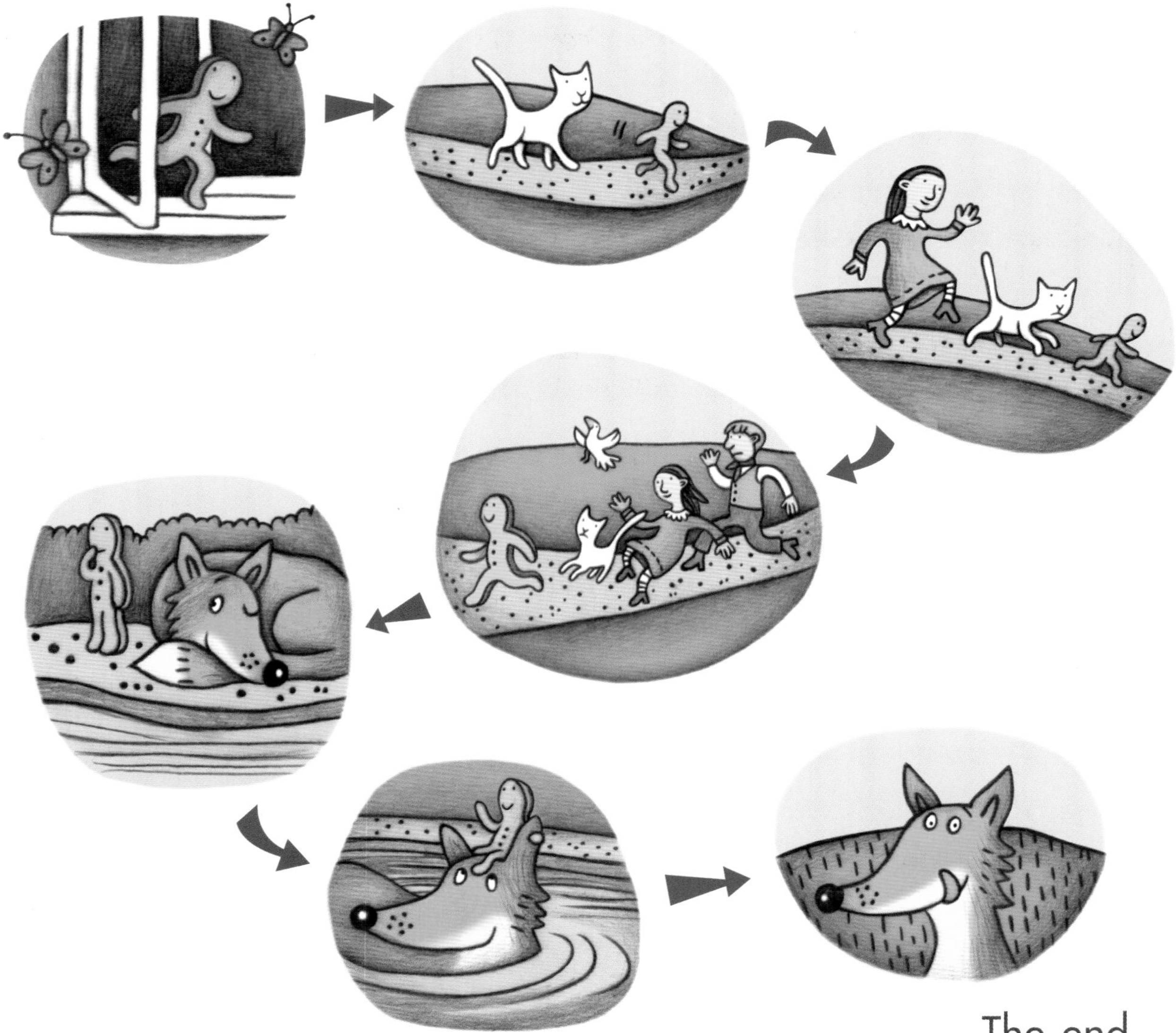

The end.